The Last
Christmas Tree

STEPHEN
KRENSKY

illustrated by

PASCAL
CAMPION

Almost exactly a month before Christmas,
the trees arrived for the holiday.
On the day before, the lot had been empty.

Now it was full to bursting.
The difference was almost like magic.

There were balsam firs, spruces and pines,
all lined up neatly at a slight tilt.

In the middle of one row, wedged between two bushier companions, one particular tree trembled with excitement.

It was not very tall, and, in truth, a bit hunched over. Not to mention the branches that were missing here and there.

Still, no tree was more filled with
the spirit of the season. Surely,
everyone would see that at once.

The little tree could hardly wait to get picked.
What a moment that would be!

It imagined itself covered with lights and ornaments, with presents tucked in snugly underneath.

The other trees didn't seem to care about
who picked them out or how long it took.

But the little tree kept its hopes high. It wanted someone special, someone who was as excited about Christmas as it was.

As the days passed, the trees were sold one by one.
A few people made up their minds in an instant.
They knew what they wanted, and that was that.
Others went back and forth and back and forth
for what seemed like hours—and sometimes was.

One family pulled out the little tree for a
closer look. But they were laughing meanly
and shaking their heads the whole time.

The little tree was secretly glad when they
left it behind.

As time went on, the remaining trees were spread out, the better to show themselves off.

No longer hemmed in, the little tree tried to stand up straight and puff itself out as much as possible.

But nobody seemed to notice.

The lot got emptier and emptier.

The few unsold trees found their
prices marked down again and
again and again.

On Christmas Eve, the little tree looked to the left and looked to the right.

It was all alone.
A sign was hung on it in big letters.
It wasn't an ornament, not really.
But the tree chose to think otherwise.

JINGLEJINGLEJINGLEJINGLEJINGLEJINGLEJ

The night was cold and clear,
and the little tree got rather sleepy.
Just before dawn, it thought it heard
a jingling sound, but it was hard to be sure.

The next thing the tree knew, it was
gently picked up and placed in an empty sack.
This wasn't what the tree had expected at all.

Then the earth fell away. Far below,
the other trees were covered in all of their finery.
The little tree had no idea where it was
going or how long the journey would take.

But when it arrived at last . . .

. . . the little Christmas
tree was finally home.

For Peter & Nicole
—to celebrate their first married Christmas.
—S.K.

For Katrina, Lily, Max and Colin
—P.C.

DIAL BOOKS FOR YOUNG READERS
Published by the Penguin Group * Penguin Group (USA) LLC, 375 Hudson Street, New York, NY 10014

USA | Canada | UK | Ireland | Australia | New Zealand | India | South Africa | China
PENGUIN.COM

A PENGUIN RANDOM HOUSE COMPANY

Text copyright © 2014 by Stephen Krensky * Illustrations copyright © 2014 by Pascal Campion

Library of Congress Cataloging-in-Publication Data
Krensky, Stephen. * The last Christmas tree / by Stephen Krensky ; illustrated by Pascal Campion.
pages cm * Summary: An eager little Christmas tree, not very tall or well-shaped, is the last on the lot but when it seems all hope of being covered with lights and ornaments is lost, a special person comes to take him home.
ISBN 978-0-8037-3757-0 (hardcover) * [1. Christmas trees—Fiction. 2. Hope—Fiction.] I. Campion, Pascal, illustrator. II. Title.
PZ7.K883Las 2014 [E]—dc23 2013034357

Manufactured in China on acid-free paper * 10 9 8 7 6 5 4 3 2 1
Designed by Jason Henry * Text set in ITC Esprit * The artwork for this book was created digitally. * The publisher does not have any control over and does not assume any responsibility for author or third-party websites or their content.